KEEPERS OF THE VAULT

SHADOW AND SPELL

Published by Clockwise Press Inc., 56 Aurora Heights Dr.,
Aurora, ON Canada L4G2W7

www.clockwisepress.com

christie@clockwisepress.com   solange@clockwisepress.com

10 9 8 7 6 5 4 3 2 1

Library and Archives Canada Cataloguing in Publication
Information on File
Chan, Marty, author
Shadow and Spell / Marty Chan.
(Keepers of the vault ; 3)
Issued in print and electronic formats.
ISBN 978-1-988347-07-3 (paperback).
ISBN 978-1-988347-08-0 (pdf)

An ebook version of this book set in OpenDyslexia font is
available online.

Cover art by Harlee Noble
Cover and Interior design by CommTech Unlimited
The text of this book is set in Myanmar font.
Printed in Canada by Webcom

MIX
Paper from
responsible sources
FSC
www.fsc.org   FSC® C004071

KEEPERS OF THE VAULT

SHADOW AND SPELL

MARTY CHAN

CLOCKWISE
PRESS

It takes a village to raise a child. My villagers include: Christie Harkin, Kate Harkin, Wei Wong, Solange Messier, and Michelle Chan.
Thanks for all your help.

M.C.

1 : The Lost Page

I didn't know which kept more secrets: the vault or the keeper of the vault.

Mr. Grimoire had been acting even more strangely than usual ever since Anji and I had recovered the artefacts that his former apprentice Rebecca had stolen. Aleister Crowley's *Book of Spells* was back on the shelf with the other dusty books. The enchanted music box was safely locked in its cabinet. The bag of Dragon Teeth was tucked away behind something that looked like a crocodile skull.

Everything was back in its place, exactly as it should be.

Still, Mr. Grimoire continued to check and double-check the collection of ancient curiosities that were under his care. He examined the locks on display cases, sifted through chests full of valuable trinkets, and counted all the items in the vault. If ever Dylan or Anji or I tried to help, he'd just wave us off, like we were annoying mosquitoes instead of his apprentices who'd already risked their lives for him and his artefacts.

Today, he decided to take down the *Book of Spells*.

"Can I get you a cup of tea, sir?" I asked as he flipped through the pages.

"No. I'm fine."

I leaned closer.

"Is there anything I can do to help, Mr. Grimoire?"

He covered the pages with his arms. "Sure, Kristina. Why don't you count the Yellow Emperor's Dragon Teeth?"

"Okay. There should be thirty-six, right?"

"Yes. Thirty-six." His arms remained resting on the pages and his gaze locked on me until I backed away from whatever secret spell he was reading.

I sighed as I picked up the black pouch from the table and poured out the gnarled yellow fangs. The odour punched up my nose.

Anji and Dylan crowded around the table. She pulled her black hair into a ponytail while he rolled up the sleeves of his plaid shirt.

Dylan waved the stink away. "Oh, man. They smell worse than my cousin's hockey bag at the end of the season."

"Why would Rebecca steal these?" asked Anji.

"If you plant one of these teeth, you can grow

twelve warriors every full moon," I explained. Anji was still pretty new at this apprentice job. "Rebecca could literally have grown herself an army to have at her command."

"Now we're stuck counting these stinky things," said Dylan. "Maybe we should grow the soldiers and make them take a bath."

Anji laughed.

"Don't encourage him," I said. "He'll never stop."

"Well, it's the least they could do for us after we went to the trouble of saving them."

"We?" I said. "Dylan, I don't remember you risking your life in Rebecca's grandmother's house."

"I was there in spirit," he said. "Plus, I helped carry her luggage to the cab."

Anji snickered. "Yeah, the hero always helps the old lady to the airport."

"Hey, if I could have been with you guys, maybe we could have managed to actually catch Rebecca."

"Anji's trolling you, Dylan."

"I knew that," he mumbled as he pushed a dragon tooth back and forth on the table. "Do you think Rebecca will join her grandmother in Victoria?"

"No idea. I hope so."

"Don't count on it," Mr. Grimoire growled. "My former apprentice is up to no good."

I hastily swept the teeth into the bag. "All done!" I said brightly. "Thirty-six teeth, as expected. So, what's next?"

Truth was, the subject of Rebecca and her escape wasn't something I wanted to dwell on. Like Mr. Grimoire, I had secrets to keep. Sure, Rebecca had stolen the book, the teeth, and Dr. Von Himmel's Music Box. But when I learned that she was trying to raise money to help her ailing grandmother, and once I met her face to face, I was pretty sure she wasn't the evil villain Mr. Grimoire made her out to be.

So I'd let her escape.

Suddenly, Mr. Grimoire slammed his hand on the book. "No! This book is missing a page!"

"What? Are you sure?" I asked as the three of us rushed to his side.

Mr. Grimoire stabbed at the loose stitching in the middle of the book.

"Maybe the page was missing before," Dylan suggested. "After all, it's a pretty old book."

"No, they were stitched securely into the spine of the book. I've read it many times. This is a recent loss. See the loose strands of hair? And the fragment of human hide?"

I had to choke back the bitter taste of bile at the back of my throat. "The book was made of skin?"

He nodded.

"Do you know which spell is missing?" Anji asked.

He closed the book. "A summoning spell. With it, Rebecca can bring forth the Nightshades."

"You mean those weed things with the purple flowers and poison berries?" I asked.

He shook his head. "Aleister Crowley was a warlock with knowledge of the dark magical arts. He discovered an ancient scroll from the Deristos, a civilization that time has since erased. The scroll allowed Deristosian dark magicians to summon deadly creatures from the netherworld. These dark forms had substance but could hide within the shadows. The Deristosians called them Nightshades. These creatures were able to sneak into enemy fortresses, assassinate rulers, and defeat those who stood against them. The Nightshades work best in dark alleys where few eyes can see. Imagine your own shadow rising up to destroy you."

"If they're so powerful, what happened to them? Why haven't we heard of Deristos or Nightshades?" Anji asked.

"They were defeated by a group of warriors who could command light. According to legend, these warriors used piercing light to banish the Nightshades back to the netherworld."

Dylan let out a low whistle. "Okay, flashlights for everyone."

Mr. Grimoire walked over to a glass case that displayed a rack of gems. He lifted the lid and retrieved a few gems. "These are Star Crystals. They are what the warriors used against the Nightshades. They will ward off the creatures."

He handed one gem to each of us. The golf ball sized crystal felt lighter than I thought it should have been. The surface was smooth and warm in my hand.

"How do we make the crystals work?" I asked.

Mr. Grimoire held a crystal in his hand and said, "*Ku-fi-laz.*"

Light exploded from his hand, blinding me temporarily. The heat of the Star Crystal's light blasted against my cheeks.

"*Hap-wisk,*" Mr. Grimoire said. The light and heat faded away.

"Wow!" Dylan said. "Great party trick."

"The Star Crystals are not for fun," Mr. Grimoire scolded. "Use them only if you have to. They only have so much power. Then you have to recharge them in the sunlight. Understood?"

We nodded.

"Mr. Grimoire, we can't be sure that Rebecca has the missing page," I said. "Why don't we search around her grandmother's house and see if it might have fallen out of the book?"

"I know Rebecca has it," Mr. Grimoire said. "By now she's probably summoned the Nightshades."

"For all we know, the page is mixed in with somebody's recycling," Anji suggested.

"I'm with Mr. Grimoire," Dylan said. "We can't trust Rebecca."

"What could it hurt to look for the spell?" argued Anji. "If we're wrong, what do we lose?"

Mr. Grimoire folded his arms over his chest. "It's a waste of time. Rebecca has the page and she's probably delivered it to that collector, Lenore Frobisher. We know that the two of them are in league together to get at the contents of this vault."

"Look, Anji and I can go back to the house to look for the spell page," I said.

"It's been a week since we recovered the artefacts," he pointed out.

"We should still look. Meanwhile, Dylan can stay here and help you secure the entrances to the vault in case I'm wrong. That way we can cover all our bases."

"Fine," Mr. Grimoire said in a huff. "But if you

don't find anything by nightfall, we will have to assume that Rebecca is behind this."

I nodded. Anji and I headed out of the vault. The instant teleportation that magically transitioned us from the hidden room on the fourth floor to our normal school hallway always made me want to puke. But I kept my lunch down.

On the bus ride to Rebecca's grandmother's house, Anji surfed on her smartphone while I stared out the window at the passing houses, chewing my bottom lip. Mr. Grimoire seemed so certain that Rebecca was up to no good, but the Rebecca he knew was not like the one I had met.

She seemed more desperate than greedy. I had used Dr. Von Himmel's music box to take control of her mind. Under the spell, she had to do everything I asked. I demanded she tell me why she stole from Mr. Grimoire. Her answer? She wanted to raise enough money to pay for her sick grandmother's experimental medical treatments.

We walked from the bus stop to the house where we had our last showdown with Rebecca and Lenore. Then we combed the immediate area for any sign of the missing page. It was a quiet street with rows of bungalows edged with hedges and picket fences: lots of great hiding places for stray pieces of paper to get caught up in.

Anji turned to me. "What is it with Mr. Grimoire? He has a full hate-on for Rebecca."

I shrugged. "No idea."

"I guess I'd be ticked too, like if someone hacked into my computer."

"This seems like something more. It's almost like it's personal."

"Reminds me of my uncle when someone broke into his house. After that, he didn't trust anyone. Called the cops on kids walking down the street at night. Stared out his window with a baseball bat in his lap until two in the morning. At one point, my mom had to talk him out of getting guard dogs."

"So what finally got him to calm down?" I asked.

"Nothing. He's still wound up, and it's been two years."

"Wow. Let's hope Mr. Grimoire doesn't go down that road."

Anji nodded. I peered into neighbours' yards. I had hoped the page might have blown against a tree or under a car, but with a week gone by, the chances of finding it were as likely as the chances of my dad mailing my mom a grocery cheque these days.

We moved to the next street. Plenty of trash but no page.

"What's that?"

I rushed over to where Anji was pointing and picked up a piece of paper. One quick scan of some poor handwriting and bad spelling told me what I had found.

"It's a kid's homework assignment."

"Probably just as well that he lost it. That is some terrible handwriting, and look at the spelling mistakes."

"You're a natural-born teacher, Anji."

She faked a bow with a grand gesture then glanced up. "The sun's going down. Think we should call off the search?"

"One more street," I begged.

"My parents will wonder what's wrong with me if they don't see me glued to the computer monitor at home. They might even think I have a social life. Shudder."

I laughed. "My mom's been out a lot, so she never notices what time I get home these days."

"Poor you. You need an edgy soundtrack of tragedy," Anji said.

I chuckled. "I'd better check in with Mr. Grimoire. Tell him we had no luck."

"I'm sure he'll love the chance to say, 'I told you so.'"

As we strolled through the suburbs on the way

back to the bus stop, I studied the quiet houses. One bungalow reminded me of my old home on the south side. I missed my room. I missed my yard. I missed the Sunday mornings I spent with Mom and Dad making pancakes together. I missed being a family.

Anji elbowed my side, poking me out of the daydream.

"What's wrong?" I asked.

"I think we're being followed."

2: WATCHERS

Anji gripped my wrist so tightly I thought she was going to break it. She half-walked, half-dragged me to the end of the block.

"Slow down," I said. "I don't see anyone behind us."

Her grip relaxed. I glanced over my shoulder. A light blue minivan was parked on the side of the street.

"There's no one there," I said.

"Farther back."

I glanced back again and spotted a four-door black sedan parked under a tree.

"The black car? What about it? It's just sitting there."

"No. That car has always been behind us. When we were down the other block, I saw it parked across the road. At first, I thought it was my imagination, but every block we went to, the car was always there."

"Are you sure it's the same one?"

"Positive."

I glanced at the vehicle again. "You're paranoid."

She yanked me around the corner and broke into a sprint. About halfway down, she motioned me to duck behind a hedged fence. We squeezed into a corner and pressed our backs against the wooden gate. She peered around the hedge then jumped back.

"I was right."

"Is it there?" I asked.

"Peek out. Not too far."

I leaned out. The black car rolled around the corner and parked about a quarter of the way down the road.

"You believe me now?"

"It does seem suspicious."

"Maybe they want to follow us to the vault."

"Maybe."

She fished out her phone and turned on the camera app. She aimed it at the car and swiped her finger and thumb across the screen. The camera zoomed in, but the tinted windshield masked the driver inside.

"Rats. Can't see who it is," she said and pocketed her phone. "They don't know we're onto them. Let's keep it that way, Kristina. Follow me." She stepped out from the hedged fence and walked away from the car.

"Keep up and get ready to run," she said.

She pretended to search for the missing page. I followed suit, but I kept one eye on the car and one hand on the Star Crystal in my jeans pocket. My legs felt rubbery. Ahead, Anji's long black hair whipped in the wind.

"When we get to the corner, I'll go left. You go right."

"What?" I asked.

"They can't catch both of us."

Before I could question the wisdom of her plan, Anji broke into a sprint. Tires screeched behind me. The black car sped toward us. With no time to argue, I just ran. Halfway down the street, I spotted a house with a light on and sped toward it.

The car swerved around the corner and barrelled after me. I couldn't get to the safe house in time. Instead, I veered to the right and ran to a narrow path between two empty houses. If they wanted me, they'd have to follow on foot. I dashed to the backyard.

Woof!

I skidded to a stop and came face to teeth with a big dog. The German Shepherd barked at me, straining at the chain holding him to the stake in the yard. I backed away, but the sound of a car door stopped me. Footsteps hurried toward me. I was trapped.

I scanned the narrow pathway for a weapon. Other than a straw doormat and a couple of empty flower pots, I was pretty much defenseless. The only two options before me were the dog or the driver. I advanced on the dog.

He snarled and barked as I inched around the perimeter of the yard. I aimed for the chain-link fence at the far end of the yard, hoping to get there before the person from the car could catch me.

I skirted past the dog. He lunged at me once more, pulling at the chain that held him to the stake. I squeezed against the fence, trying to shrink away from the dog's teeth. Then the dog turned and growled at something near the side of the house.

A shadow moved toward us, growing in size and taking the shape of a human giant. This had to be the Nightshade. I fumbled in my pocket for the Star Crystal and pulled it out just as the creature reached the dog.

"*Ku-fi-laz!*"

Light burst from my hand and lit up the yard. It wasn't a Nightshade. The shadow turned out to be a large, muscular woman shielding her eyes against the glare. She lowered her arm to give me a clear view of her face.

My jaw nearly dropped to the ground. It

was the nurse who'd been helping Rebecca's grandmother at the house.

The burly woman flexed her muscles and lumbered toward me, taking no notice of the dog now snapping at her.

"You're coming with me," she said.

"Who are you? What do you want?"

"Tell Grimoire that Lenore Frobisher sends her greetings."

"You're Lenore?"

She cracked a grim smile and closed the gap between us. The dog lunged at her.

I dived onto the grass and slid to the metal stake. With both hands, I grabbed the stake and pulled, gritting my teeth. The stake wouldn't budge at first. I pulled harder, getting leverage with my elbows on the wet grass. The stake popped out and flew out of my hands.

I rolled onto my back just in time to see the dog slam his paws into Lenore's chest and drive her against the house. I scrambled to the back of the yard and climbed over the tall fence, leaving Lenore to wrestle with the snarling dog.

I ran down the alley and retraced my steps to the street where Anji and I had split up, then headed in the direction my friend had run.

There was no sign of her anywhere. I jogged

along the row of houses, looking left and right, holding the Star Crystal up to ward off any supernatural followers.

Suddenly, a hand grabbed my arm. I shrieked, but another hand clamped over my mouth.

"*Shh*," Anji hissed.

I nodded, glad to see my friend alive and well.

"That was a terrible plan, Anji."

"You got away, didn't you? Want to turn off the light? It's killing my eyes."

"*Hap-wisk.*"

The light faded.

"Lenore Frobisher was the one in the car. She's the one following us."

"Did you see any Nightshades?"

I shook my head. "I don't think so."

Anji scanned the streets as she pulled out her Star Crystal. "We don't want to attract too much attention to ourselves, but better to be safe than sorry."

Police sirens wailed in the night. A cop car turned the corner and screeched to a halt in front of us.

Anji pointed frantically down the street as the officer climbed out of the vehicle.

"Are you Deena?" she asked.

"Yes, yes. The black car is halfway down the

block. I don't know how many were in the car, but they're after a kid. Hurry!"

I added. "It was a woman. She looked like a bodybuilder."

The cop climbed back in the car and roared down the street.

"Who's Deena?" I asked.

"You think I'd give my real name? Let's get out of here."

We ran to the bus stop and waited. Darkness settled in around us, but some of the shadows near the stop seemed darker than the others. I had the creepy feeling that something or someone was watching me. A shadow moved to the right of me, and I grabbed the Star Crystal out of my pocket.

"What's up, Kristina?"

The shadow moved again.

"*Ku-fi-laz*!" I chanted as I raised the crystal over my head. Light burst from my hand and flooded the street. A screech floated into the night as the shadowy figure slinked away.

"Was that... could it have been... what *was* that?"

I shook my head. "I think it might have been a Nightshade."

"It was watching us. Who sent it? Lenore or Rebecca?"

"I don't know, Anji, but I don't want to stick around to find out. *Hap-wisk.*" The light faded from my Star Crystal.

A few minutes later, a bus rolled up and Anji and I got on board. I glanced back at the street, hoping to see the cops drive by with Lenore handcuffed in the back seat. No such luck.

On the ride, Anji scanned her phone for any information about our enemy. I peeked at her screen as the bus rolled through the residential neighbourhood.

"According to this business article, Lenore inherited a steel manufacturing empire," Anji said. "Apparently, she had a twin sister, but she died in a car accident along with their parents. Lenore was the sole heir to the family fortune."

"Someone that rich must be used to getting what she wants," I said.

"Maybe that's why she's so keen on the stuff in the vault. Mr. Grimoire won't let her have it."

I grinned. "You might be right. At least now we know for sure that the spell page isn't missing. Someone stole it and used it to summon a Nightshade. Think it was Rebecca or Lenore?"

"Had to be Lenore," I said. "It's no coincidence that she was watching us."

"Why didn't she send the Nightshade after you?"

"I don't know. The Nightshade was at the bus stop. Maybe it was following you."

Anji chewed the bottom of her lip. "I was the target?"

"Maybe."

"Do you think Rebecca sold Lenore the spell?"

I tapped my fingers on my leg, trying to make sense of it all. Was I wrong about Rebecca? Why would she sell the spell to Lenore? Only Rebecca could answer this question and I had no idea where she was.

"Doesn't matter," I said. "Lenore is the one we have to worry about now."

"Yes, but Kristina, if Rebecca is working for her, she'll know all the weak spots in the vault's security."

I couldn't argue against my friend's logic. "Okay, we have to warn Mr. Grimoire," I said.

When we arrived at the school, the building was closed. Mr. Grimoire kept a master key hidden in the crossbar of the bike stand near the west side of the building. I unscrewed the cap at the end and fished out the metal key. I opened the side

24

door while Anji scanned the schoolyard with her Star Crystal at the ready. Once inside, we trekked up the flights of stairs to the fourth floor.

I tugged on the chain that looped through the door handles at the top of the stairs three times, knocked on the left door twice, and then whistled four short bursts. No one responded. I tried again. Still nothing.

"You sure you're doing it right?" Anji asked.

Scratching my head, I peered through the glass at the empty storage area on the other side. "Positive."

I tried one more time. Still no change. We were locked out.

"Well, it looks as if Mr. Grimoire doesn't want us to come in," Anji said.

"Hold on. I have an idea." I fished a piece of chalk out of my pocket. "Mr. Grimoire gave me this to communicate with him inside the vault."

"Be easier if he had a phone and could text."

"Definitely, but we'll take what we can get." I scrawled a message on the floor:

We are here. Let us in.

Anji and I waited for a few minutes, then I tried the door again. Nothing.

"I guess he's taking no chances."

"Weird," I said, scratching my head.

"Either that or you really ticked him off."

I shrugged. "I'm sure Dylan will know the way in. Let's call it a night."

"Yeah. Nothing else we can do tonight, and if we can't get in, I doubt Rebecca or Lenore will be able to."

We left the building and made our way to the bus stop. I took one last look behind me as our bus pulled up. Just as I looked away, I thought I saw a flash of light erupt from the fourth floor out of the corner of my eye.

I hesitated for a moment. Had I really seen something? If so, should we go back and investigate? If not, did I really want to be stuck here for another hour in the dark, waiting for the next bus for no reason?

We climbed on, but I kept staring back at the school. No more bursts of light. What was up there? I scanned the streets, still unable to shake the creepy feeling that someone was watching me.

3: Locked Out

At the closet pretending to be my mom's apartment, I pulled open the sofa bed and grabbed my sheet. Mom worked at the kitchen table, which doubled as both a desk and general storage area for her homework, my school books, and our dirty dishes. She sifted through papers while I spread my sheet and blanket across the lumpy mattress.

"Mom, can you turn out the light? I need to go to sleep."

"Another minute, Kristina. I'm trying to sort something out."

"Can I help?"

She shook her head. "Not unless you have a winning lottery ticket."

I smoothed out the sheet. "What's the matter, Mom?"

"Nothing for you to worry about."

She painted on a thin-lipped smile, which I recognized all too well. It was the same fake grin she gave me when she told me that she and Dad were getting a divorce and that it was all going to be okay. I dropped the pillow on the bed and joined Mom at the kitchen-desk-storage table.

She had been going through bills and a bank statement with a pen. She had marked up the bank statement with the total of the bills and circled the bank balance. The bill amount was higher than the balance.

"Are we in trouble?" I asked.

"We're going to be okay."

"Mom, please don't do that."

"Do what?"

"Protect me from bad news like I'm eight years old. I can see that we're short of money."

"It's not that bad. I'll hold off on paying the credit card this month and pay the late fee."

"What happened to the money? I thought we were saving some by moving into this apartment."

She nodded. "So did I, but I didn't count on my boss cutting back my hours this month."

"What about Dad's money? Isn't he supposed to be giving you something every month?"

"Don't worry. We'll be okay. You need to get to bed and I need to get to work early." She flashed another thin-lipped smile.

"Dad is paying his share, right? He promised he would."

"Go to sleep, Kristina. We'll talk in the morning."

She turned off the lamp and shuffled to the bedroom. I climbed into my bed. As I pulled the blanket over myself, I wondered if this meant we had to find an even smaller apartment. I shuddered.

The next morning, Mom headed to work while I was in the shower. I got the feeling she was avoiding me. I poured a bowl of cereal but stopped and put half of the cereal back in the box, thinking that I might want to ration the food. Instead of milk, I poured tap water into the bowl. As I munched the bland flakes, I wondered how bad our finances were and if Dad knew about this. I washed the bowl and headed to school.

Dylan and Anji were waiting for me in the schoolyard. I glanced over my shoulder to search for any sign of the Nightshades. Nothing.

"I told Dylan about your run-in with Lenore Frobisher."

"So, Mr. Grimoire was right. Rebecca is working with Lenore."

"We don't know that for sure, Dylan," I said. "Rebecca's name never came up. All we know is that Lenore is in the picture."

"We'd better tell him about this."

"We tried last night, but the entrance didn't work."

"Oh yeah, right. We changed things around while you two were looking for the missing page. There's a different way in now."

"Where is it?"

He glanced over his shoulder at the other students in the hallway. No one was paying attention to us, but he scanned their shadows. "I can't tell you here. Not out loud. In case any You-Know-Whats might be listening in on us."

"Oh," I said. "Okay."

"Mr. Grimoire is taking no chances. We set up an eye in the sky to watch the fourth floor in case anyone tried to get in."

"Eye in the sky? What's that?" I asked.

"He put an eyeball in the ceiling. A real eye. Get this. Mr. Grimoire had a box full of them."

"Glass eyeballs?" I asked.

"Nope. I picked one up. It was squishy and it stared at me no matter where I walked."

"*Ew.*" I winced.

"Cool. How does it work?" Anji asked. Clearly, this was right up her hacker-internet-spy alley.

"There's a crystal ball that's connected to the eye. You can look in and see whatever the eye is seeing."

Her smile dropped. "Oh. I was hoping for something cool, like, you plug your brain into it."

"The weird thing was after we installed it, we saw something was trying to get into the vault."

"Yeah. That was us."

He shook his head. "No, Kristina. I saw your message. I checked on the crystal ball and saw you there. I was about to let you in when Mr. Grimoire spotted something behind you. We were going to rescue you, but you went down the stairs and the shadow stayed at the door. Mr. Grimoire cracked the portal open a sliver and blasted the thing with the Star Crystal, except it didn't destroy it. The Nightshade just backed away from the light."

"The same thing happened when we came across one in the backyard," I said. "The Star Crystals don't seem to be strong enough to banish the creatures back to the netherworld."

"After that, Mr. Grimoire cut off the fourth-floor entrance and started looking for another weapon to destroy the Nightshades."

"So, how do we get into the vault, Dylan?" Anji asked impatiently.

"I told you. It's not safe to say. Meet me at lunch by the bike racks. I have to get to class."

We split off. I grabbed books from my locker and headed to language arts class. Mr. Carlton skipped in with the enthusiasm of a kindergarten teacher on a sugar rush. He had been in good spirits ever since he announced he was retiring at the end of the school year to promote his first published novel. I was going to miss Mr. Carlton, but the other students couldn't care less.

"Today, we're going to focus on the persuasive essay," he said.

Groans filled the air.

"No need to despair. By the time I'm finished *persuading* you about the power of the persuasive essay, you're going to be on your feet and cheering."

"Unlikely," a boy called out from the back.

"Essays are boring," another student added.

Our teacher shook his head. "Those are personal observations. Good for colour, but you've got to back them up with some statistics. See if you can find evidence that the essay can lull people to sleep. Or is it the natural state of a teenager to always be groggy in English class?"

He rapped on the back of the head of a boy who was using his backpack as a pillow.

"Two more minutes, Mom."

Mr. Carlton pulled the backpack away.

The boy clung to the backpack strap. "Hey, my homework's in there."

"You? Finishing your work and bringing it to school? That would be as likely as me setting foot on Mars."

The others laughed as Mr. Carlton bounced back to the front of the room.

"Don't judge an essay by the first impression. Sometimes, you have to dig deeper to find the real face of something. When you do, it may change your attitude."

Our teacher launched into the structure of the essay, but a movement at the edge of the room caught my eye.

I turned. Something looked odd about Dylan. More specifically, something looked odd about the shadow he cast against the classroom wall. Maybe I was being paranoid, but it seemed to me as though the other students' shadows were faded and dim, while Dylan's seemed darker and higher on the wall.

For a second, I thought the shadow had moved on its own, but it was Dylan shifting in his desk as Mr. Carlton walked between the desks toward me.

"Kristina, I see you find it more interesting to watch paint peel from the old classroom wall."

I spun around in my desk. "No, sir. I was just... Never mind."

"It's okay, Kristina. Sometimes, I daydream, too. Especially when I'm thinking about what to write for my next book. You all know that I'm getting published, right?"

Groans around the room. Mr. Carlton never failed to mention his new career in every class. Some days, he plugged his new book three or four times.

"Have I said this before?"

The students in unison answered, "Yes."

"Then *persuade* me to stop with your essays."

I glanced back at Dylan's shadow on the wall, but it seemed to have returned to normal. I searched the room for any abnormal shadows. Everything seemed fine.

By the end of class, I was a rat's nest of nerves. I shot up from my desk and grabbed Dylan by the arm. "Careful of the Nightshades," I whispered.

He stiffened and glanced around. We headed into the hallway with the rest of the students. I gripped the Star Crystal in my pocket as Dylan and I made our way to our lockers to find Anji.

Lunchtime in the school hallway was chaos. Imagine caging a herd of feral cats for two hours then setting them free. A couple of gawky boys nearly hit a teacher in the face with their gangly arms waving around. A short girl ping-ponged from one student to the other as she tried to get to her locker. Kids slammed locker doors closed and banged into each other in the crowded hallway as they tried to find their lunch spot.

I didn't know why they were in such a rush. Every kid picked the exact same spot every day. No one ever changed where they sat. It was almost like they had been so used to getting assigned seats in class that they naturally assigned themselves to spots along the hallway.

Anji lingered by the front entrance of the school, watching us. I signalled her to be quiet and glanced over my shoulder. She raised an eyebrow but said nothing. Instead, she pushed open the door and stepped into the sunlight. Dylan followed as I pulled out my Star Crystal.

"*Ku-fi-laz*," I whispered.

The light burst from the gem and flooded the hallway behind me. I waited for Nightshades to flee. Nothing. Some students shielded their eyes at the end of the hallway.

"*Hap-wisk.*"

The light faded and I stepped outside.

Anji and Dylan both had their crystals in hand.

She asked, "You're sure you saw a Nightshade?"

I shook my head. "Not sure, but something seemed odd in the classroom. I don't think we should take any chances."

Dylan agreed. "Mr. Grimoire said the creatures should be weaker in the daylight. The Star Crystals might have a stronger effect on them."

"Let's hope for our sake they do," Anji said.

4: THE SEARCH

Dylan led us off the school grounds and into the neighbourhood. We passed old bungalows and parked cars. The old trees lined the street, casting shadows across the pavement. At one point, I thought for sure that we were walking into a trap.

After three blocks, Dylan slowed down as he approached a boarded-up grocery store on the corner of a quiet street.

"What are we doing here?" Anji asked.

"You'll see."

Dylan stopped in front of the building. He craned his neck to look up then shoved his hand in his jeans pocket and pulled out the golf ball–sized Star Crystal, motioning us to do the same. I scanned the neighbourhood for any Nightshades.

"What's the matter?" Anji asked.

Dylan pointed at the boarded-up window. "Look."

I shook my head. "I don't see anything."

He sprinted over to the storefront and pointed up at the eavestrough. Something round hung from a wire or string. Anji and I ventured closer to the thing. An eyeball dangled from a vein attached to the gutter.

I recoiled from the sight. "Gross!"

Dylan shook his head. "It's one of the eyes in the sky I had to put up last night at the entrance. It was supposed to be hidden above the gutter so it could watch for intruders. Someone found it."

He reached up and plucked the eyeball from the vein. The eyeball had been smushed like a flattened grape.

"Do you think a magpie spotted it and tried to eat it?" Anji asked.

Dylan examined the eye more closely. "I don't think so. A bird would have pecked at it and probably eaten the whole thing. This looks like someone crushed it."

"Do you think the entrance is compromised?"

"Only one way to find out." He lifted the Star Crystal, motioning us to do the same with ours. "Let's make sure none of those things are around."

"*Ku-fi-laz*!" we shouted in unison.

Light burst from the gems and flooded the storefront and street around it. We were bathed in a white piercing light. I shielded my eyes and squinted around for any sign of Nightshades. Nothing moved. Part of me hoped the crystals were working; another part of me feared they did not work at all. After a few minutes, we lowered our crystals and commanded them to turn off.

Dylan then turned to the boarded-up window and tapped on the middle board seven times. He muttered, "*Wence, wint, wick*" three times before tracing a star pattern out of the nails in the bottom board. He stepped back. Nothing happened.

"I might have screwed up. I'll try again." He repeated the ritual a second and a third time, but nothing happened. We were locked out of the vault.

"Are you sure you have everything in the right order?"

"Yes, Kristina. Mr. Grimoire made me go over it a hundred times to get it right."

"Then he must have changed the password," Anji suggested. "The question is why?"

"I'll bet it has to do with whatever took down the eye in the sky," Dylan guessed. "Now we're never going to get into the vault."

"Wait. I think I still have the chalk Mr. Grimoire gave us." I reached into my back pocket and fished out the white stick.

"Great. Tell him to open the portal."

"Relax, Dylan. I've got this." I knelt down and scrawled a message on the pavement, wearing the chalk to a nub about half the length of my pinky. I stood up and examined my work.

We are at the portal. Let us in.

Dylan cocked his head to one side. "Your handwriting sucks."

I offered him the chalk. "Care to do better?"

He waved it off.

Anji paced back and forth in front of the boarded-up store. Several minutes passed. Nothing opened.

Dylan grabbed the chalk and knelt down to write another message:

It's Dylan, Kristina, and Anji. We want in.

He pocketed the chalk. A few minutes passed. Still nothing opened.

"Maybe Mr. Grimoire couldn't read your handwriting," said Anji with a smirk.

I laughed. "Foiled by horrible penmanship."

Anji shrugged. "I repeat: If he had a phone, we wouldn't have to waste our time with chalk."

"I'm not sure if cell phone service covers interdimensional space," I said.

Fifteen minutes later, we gave up, finished

our lunches, and returned to school.

Dylan scratched his head. "I don't know why he locked us out. Do you think Rebecca broke into the vault?"

I shook my head. "I don't think so."

"Why not? I mean something took down the eye. Who else would have known about this portal? We need to check in on the vault and make sure it's secure—and that Mr. Grimoire is safe."

I imagined the keeper of the vault lying face down on the marble floor while Nightshades looted the vault and took the rest of its treasures. "It had to have been a Nightshade that tried to get in. You said you saw one last night."

"We won't know for sure who's behind this until we get into the vault," Anji pointed out. "And it doesn't look like we're going to get access anytime soon."

"What if we find Rebecca?" I said. "If we track her down, we can get the truth out of her."

"What good would that do?"

"Dylan, you and Mr. Grimoire think she's still trying to get the treasures from the vault for Lenore Frobisher. If she is, we can stop her. If she isn't, maybe she could be helpful."

Anji shrugged. "I'm for it. Nothing else we can do in the meantime."

"I guess. But Kristina, I don't get it. Why do you keep sticking up for her?"

I couldn't tell them my reasons. "I just don't think she's as bad as Mr. Grimoire says, that's all. And we're going to need all the help we can get if we're going to get into the vault."

"Maybe...we'll see," Dylan said slowly. Then he turned to Anji. "So, do you think you can track down her address?"

"I might be able to work some magic," Anji said. "I'll have to get on a computer. Give me to the end of the school day."

The rest of the day dragged on. I barely paid attention in class. My mind kept wandering to the vault and wondering what might have happened to Mr. Grimoire. Part of me feared that he had been attacked, but another part of me wondered if he had lost trust in us and was locking us out on purpose. Either way, I knew the only way forward was to find Rebecca and get her to help us.

Dylan and I found Anji outside her usual haunt, the school library, with a laptop perched on her knees as she typed. She barely glanced up at us as we sat beside her.

"Any progress?" I asked.

"I have the five addresses of her old foster homes."

"Isn't that stuff supposed to be private, Anji?"

She smiled at Dylan. "I haven't seen a firewall that I can't break through, yet."

"Okay. We can check out the addresses," I said.

"Do you think she's actually going to go back to her foster families?"

I shrugged. "Who knows? At the very least we can talk to the families and find out if there's any place where Rebecca liked to hang out. It'll give us a starting point."

We headed to the most recent home on Anji's list. Our search took us to my old neighbourhood. I felt a strange sense of confidence mixed with déjà vu as we took the familiar bus route to my old house, having travelled it so many times before.

We hopped off and I led the way to the foster house, hoping to catch a glimpse of my old friends somewhere along the way. I wasn't sure if they'd recognize me anymore. I wondered if they even missed me.

Bratty kids wheeled bikes around us, pretending to herd us like cattle. Anji shot a death glare at them and they scattered as if they had just come across a horror-story clown in the woods.

"You have a way with kids," Dylan said.

"Two years of babysitting my brother."

We stopped at our destination. The quiet bungalow with a neatly mowed lawn and a couple of scattered toys looked no different than any other house on the block. I half expected to see a rundown orphanage from the movie *Annie*. I'd assumed foster homes were going to be scary places, but this was a normal house.

Anji knocked on the front door. A few minutes later, a woman answered. In her floral dress, she looked like she was heading out to a summer party. A toddler clung to one of her legs like Velcro.

"Yes? Can I help you?"

"Hi, Mrs. Thompson, don't you recognize us?" Anji asked.

The woman narrowed her gaze, puzzled.

"Rebecca's friends: Anji, Kristina, and Dylan."

"You seem a bit young to be her friends."

"We used to hang out at the mall with her. Remember that one time, we saw you shopping with her."

Though her eyes didn't register any recognition, the woman faked a smile and replied. "Oh yes. Now I remember. Of course. How are you?"

I nodded at Anji, playing along with her trick.

"We're good," I said. "We didn't mean to bother you, but Rebecca gave us some books a while back, and, well, I kind of forgot about them until now. I'm trying to return them to her."

Mrs. Thompson laughed. "Rebecca let you have one of her books? I'm surprised. She loved collecting books. Couldn't afford them all, but she read whatever she could get her hands on. Thank goodness for the local library."

"Do you see her anymore, Mrs. Thompson?" I asked.

"No. Sorry. I haven't seen her since she moved back in with her grandmother."

"Too bad. I guess I'll hang onto the books until I see her again."

We left the house and headed to the bus stop.

"How did you know she'd believe we were Rebecca's friends?"

Anji beamed. "I figured the number of foster kids this woman must have had, she wasn't going to be able to keep tabs on all their friends. Just had to feed her enough information that she'd believe we knew Rebecca."

"I'll have to remember that trick. So, what's our next move?"

"You heard the lady. Rebecca loves hanging out at the library. Let's go."

Dylan checked his phone. "Uh... guys, it's getting late. Can we pick this up tomorrow? My mom said she was picking up fried chicken for dinner tonight."

"Are you serious?" Anji asked. "You're choosing fried chicken over our investigation?"

"Actually, I wouldn't mind calling it a night," I said. "It's my weekend to stay with my dad and he's picking me up."

Dylan added, "Besides, Saturday will give us more time to search. Can you get away for a bit or will your dad want you there the whole time?"

"Nah, it'll be fine. Trust me. Let's meet at the school first thing in the morning. We'll try to get into the vault first. If Mr. Grimoire isn't answering, we'll look for Rebecca."

As we headed toward the bus stop, I thought I spotted something moving across the street. The kids were long gone, but I thought for sure I saw a person or a shadow slip in between the houses. Had the Nightshades found us? I shivered slightly and picked up the pace.

5: Family Matters

Mom had picked up a night shift at work, leaving me to wait for Dad by myself. I think she'd deliberately taken the shift to avoid him. While the relationship between Dad and me had improved since we'd reconnected, he and Mom were a bit of a different story. Still, at least now he showed up for his appointed visits. Before, he was as unpredictable as the weather.

The intercom buzzed. I jumped up from the couch and stabbed the button. "Yes?"

"It's me. You want to come down?"

"Mom's not here if that's what you're worried about."

There was a moment of silence.

"No, sweetie. I want to show you something."

"Okay. I'll be right down."

I grabbed my suitcase and backpack then headed downstairs. He wasn't in the lobby. I stepped outside the apartment building. Dad was standing beside a shiny black pickup truck parked on the street. He waved his hand along the length of the vehicle with a flourish and cracked a smile like a cheesy showroom model.

"How do you like it?"

"Yours?"

"Picked it up yesterday. Thought you could be the first passenger. Ready to go for a ride?"

"Uh, sure."

He opened the door for me, then jogged to the driver's side and hopped in. He grabbed the steering wheel and hauled himself into the driver's seat.

"Where did you get the money to buy this?"

He beamed. "It's a lease. I'm paying in installments. You like?"

"Well, it's big."

"I need the box so I can haul my tools around."

"Business is picking up?"

He nodded. "Looks like Edmonton's in need of contractors again. Have hammer, will travel."

"You're not going up to Fort McMurray again, are you?"

He shook his head. "No more shift work. I'm running my own business. Already lined up six contracts. Mostly small home repairs, but word will spread. Hey, maybe I can get you to help me set up a Facebook page so I can promote the company."

"Sure."

"Great."

"So, things are looking up?"

"I might be able to score some better seats for the next Oilers' game. Would you like that?"

I said nothing for a bit as I pushed down my irritation at the memory of our nearly empty fridge back at the apartment. I had to ease into this.

"Dad, I'm happy with whatever seats you get as long as I can see the ice."

"Well, you'll be able to smell the players' sweat with the seats I'm going to get."

"No need to be that close."

"Did you have supper, Kristina? I thought we might go for sushi tonight."

"I'm starving. I haven't eaten anything since breakfast."

"You shouldn't skip lunch, kid."

"I had no choice. Nothing was left in the fridge."

"Your mom forget to go shopping? I guess she's too busy with her classes."

I shook my head and pursed my lips, weighing how to say what I needed to. Finally, I just decided to dive in. "Dad, we're low on money this month."

"Oh."

He stared ahead and drove.

I tried to touch the subject again. "Mom's having trouble paying the bills."

"Yeah?"

I hated when Dad resorted to one-word responses. That meant he wanted to change the subject but didn't want to be the one who changed it, so he just made it super uncomfortable until the other person dropped the matter. I wasn't going to give up.

"Have you paid Mom anything this month?"

"*Hmph.*"

"That a yes or a no?"

He gripped the steering wheel with both hands and stared at the minivan stopped in front of us.

"Dad?"

"Did your mother put you up to this?"

"No. She doesn't know anything about it. I just know that we're short of money, and I was wondering."

"She will get the money when she gets it. Tell her that."

"I'm not trying to make you out to be a bad guy. I'm sure you meant to send it... I mean, it looks like you're doing okay —"

"Kristina, I need this truck to run my business. The old minivan wasn't going to cut it. Things are tight for me, too."

"But you can still get better seats at an Oilers' game?" I shot back.

"A client offered me tickets in exchange for my cutting him a break on a job that I did. Do I have to justify how I live to you? I got enough of that from your mom and her lawyer."

"If you have the money, you should pay what you promised."

"I worked hard for this money, Kristina. I'm not just going to hand it over to your mother. What did she do to earn it?"

"You're my Dad! It's not just her. It's me, too."

He grunted and turned up the radio. We said nothing to each other for the rest of the night. At the restaurant, the only sound Dad made was chewing his sashimi and slurping his miso soup. I glared at him the entire meal. He could afford to take me out to a restaurant for a dinner, but he couldn't cough up grocery money for us.

On the way back to his place, I decided to try one more tactic: "I know you're never getting back together with Mom. I get that. But making life hard for her? And for me? Well, that's not something I thought you'd want to do."

The way the reminder landed, I could see it hit the target. His jaw tightened and he began to turn to me.

"It's complicated, Kristina. When you get older, you'll know."

"I wanted to look up to you. Now I'm not so sure."

He turned back to staring out the windshield. We rode the rest of the way in silence.

Saturday morning, Dad left a note on the kitchen table along with a hundred dollars.

"Emergency job. I'll be back later. Here's some money for breakfast and lunch. Keep the change."

I knew what Dad was up to, and I wasn't going to play along. He didn't want to give money to Mom, but he also wanted to take care of me. I left the note and the money on the table.

Anji was waiting for me outside the school. As usual, she was staring at the screen of her phone.

"Where's Dylan?" I asked.

She shrugged. "Probably slept in."

"That's not like him."

"It's Saturday."

"Can you call him and see where he is?"

She sent the text as I headed to the bike stand to retrieve the key to the school. I hoped Mr. Grimoire would see us and let us in.

"Hear anything back from Dylan yet?"

Anji shook her head. "Guess he's still sleeping."

"That's weird. Can you call his house?"

"Ugh. I hate phoning people."

I held out my hand. She tossed the phone

over and I dialed Dylan's home number.

His mom answered. "Hello?"

"Hi, Mrs. Parker. It's Kristina, Dylan's friend. Is he around?"

"Well, no. He's not with you? He left well over an hour ago and said he was going to meet you this morning."

I stiffened. "Oh, right. He must be taking his time."

"That boy is late for everything. Give him heck when you see him."

"Thanks. I will." My fingers trembled as I hung up.

"What's wrong, Kristina?"

"He left his house ages ago. He should have been here by now." I handed the phone back and sat on the front steps of the school. "Do you think the Nightshades might have gotten him?"

Anji pursed her lips. "Or maybe he found a way into the vault and is hiding out there. But you'd think he would have tried to get in touch with us, at least. Can you use that chalk to contact Mr. Grimoire?"

"Yes. Good idea."

I searched my pockets. "I had it yesterday. I know I did." I stopped midway through the search. "Dylan took it."

Anji's smile fell fast. "Right. He put it in his pocket after he scratched the message."

A horrible thought settled on my shoulders. "Do you think Lenore's holding him hostage?"

"I don't know. Shouldn't she have sent us a message?"

"Maybe she's trying to nab all of us so she can cut a deal with Mr. Grimoire." I stood up and started pacing. "We need Mr. Grimoire to help. He should at least know what's happening out here."

We went back to the side door, rushed up to the fourth floor, and tried to open the portal. No luck. Anji jumped up and down, kicking up dust, while I waved frantically at the strange eye in the sky, hoping Mr. Grimoire might see us. We waited a few minutes for any kind of response and then tried waving again. Nothing.

"Our only hope is to find Rebecca," I said. "She might know another way into the vault."

"You sure we can trust her, Kristina? I mean she did steal the stuff in the first place."

I nodded. "I can't be sure of anything, but if she's working with Lenore, capturing her is our way to getting Dylan back."

"Okay, then we'd better get to work. I wonder what the nearest library to the foster home in Mill Woods is."

"I know exactly which one." The library was only a few blocks from my old house. "Let's go!"

6: A Shadowy Encounter

"I thought tracking the real people behind anonymous Twitter accounts was fun, but this is a rush," Anji said as we travelled on the bus toward Mill Woods.

I stared out the window as we started to pass by familiar sights of my old neighbourhood again. "I have a good feeling about this one."

"You sure? What if Mr. Grimoire's right and Rebecca's working with Lenore?"

"Then we'd better be ready," I said, wishing I had more than a Star Crystal as a weapon.

We arrived at the bus stop near the local library branch. I pulled the bell cord and headed to the exit.

The library sat on the other side of a shopping mall. I stepped through the sliding doors and the familiar sight of the checkout kiosks and internet stations greeted me. The librarian behind the counter beamed. "It's been forever since I've seen you, Kristina. Where have you been?"

"We moved," I said, relieved to run into someone who remembered me.

"Well, I guess you couldn't stay away from us. What can I do for you today? Another manga?"

Anji smiled. "I didn't peg you for a graphic novel geek. *Death Note*?"

"*Tokyo Ghoul.*"

"I might have some new titles, but they rarely stay on the shelves these days," the librarian said.

"That's okay. We're looking for a friend. You might have seen her. She's a little older and taller than me. Brown hair down to her shoulders. Straight. Wears a long black coat."

"Sorry, that sounds like a lot of the people who come through the doors."

Anji added, "This person has probably been hanging out here a lot lately. Like, a *lot.*"

The librarian leaned forward and whispered, "Well, there is one young woman who's been here every day for about a week now. Shows up when the library opens and stays until we close. Today, I think she's in the nonfiction section."

I thanked the librarian and headed down the left-hand side of the stacks. Near the back of the library, a few readers sat at tables while a couple of university students studied at desks. None of my friends were here.

Anji grabbed my arm and pointed. "Is that her?"

Sitting in a chair by the window, a young woman stared out the window. I couldn't make out her face because it was turned away from us.

"I don't know. Maybe?"

"I can't see her face."

We angled our approach so we could get a better look. The woman looked over at the sound of our footsteps. She wasn't Rebecca.

I pulled Anji away. "Dead end," I whispered.

"It was a long shot, Kristina."

"Let's get out of here and figure out where else to look."

We headed out of the library, but I slowed as I reached the automatic doors that slid open. The glass reflected someone behind us. I couldn't make out the features of the woman clearly. I turned around, but she was gone.

"Anji," I said. "When we get outside, head to the bus stop. Don't look back. Just go."

"What's the matter?"

"I think we're being followed."

She reached into her pocket.

I waved her off. "Not Nightshades."

"Who then?"

"Look, you go ahead of me. If you hear me scream, run back."

She nodded. We left the building. I slowed

and slipped behind a garbage can, pretending to tie my shoe. Anji continued toward the bus stop. I peeked back at the library. No one came out of the building for several minutes. Was my imagination running wild?

Finally, the sliding doors opened and a father and his two kids shuffled out. Each of the boys lugged an armful of books. I waited a few more minutes but saw no sign of anyone suspicious.

I stood up and jogged after Anji. "Wait up."

She glanced over her shoulder and waved back at me. Her shadow cut across the pavement, but something was wrong. It seemed longer than it should have been. I paused and looked at the sky. The sun was still high.

"What's wrong?" Anji asked as she stopped.

Her shadow took a half second to stop moving. A Nightshade!

"Run!" I reached into my pocket to pull out the Star Crystal.

She bolted away from the bus shelter and down the block. The Nightshade loped after her, connected to her shadow.

I chased after them, still digging in my pocket for the Star Crystal. I finally managed to pull it out and ignited it.

"*Ku-fi-laz*!"

The light burst from my fist. I closed my fingers around the crystal to sharpen the focus and intensity like a laser beam. I hoped the concentrated light might hit the creature with enough force to banish it to the netherworld. I took aim at the Nightshade, but it was too far away. They were about a block away and moving deeper into the neighbourhood.

"Anji! Pull out your Star Crystal!"

She reached into her pocket and fumbled for the gem as she scrambled down a path into a wooded park. I lost sight of her and the Nightshade. I sprinted to the trail and followed it, still holding up the crystal, ready for any attack.

Somewhere in the trees, Anji let out a high-pitched scream.

I gave up on caution and sprinted past the trees, knocking away stray branches from my face. I burst out of the woods. Anji staggered at the water's edge. The Nightshade held her by her wrists. Her Star Crystal lay useless on the ground.

"Anji!" I ran toward her.

The darkness spread across my friend's body, engulfing her. I stabbed the Star Crystal at the Nightshade, hoping the light would chase it away, but I was still too far away.

I had to get closer. Now most of my friend's

body was covered in the Nightshade's inky form. She couldn't scream any longer because half of her face was gone. Then she blinked out and all that was left was a towering monster.

"No!"

The Nightshade doubled in size. I skidded to a stop and backed away, holding up the Star Crystal. The creature began to advance. I took another step back.

"Bring back Anji," I ordered.

The Nightshade either didn't understand or didn't care. It continued to press forward. I held the blazing Star Crystal in front of me, trying to ward off the monster. The Nightshade stopped at the edge of the light. It circled around me looking for a weakness. We were at a standoff. The Nightshade couldn't get to me and I couldn't get to Anji.

I stepped toward the pond and the Star Crystal lying on the shore. I hoped that doubling the light might drive the Nightshade away. The creature seemed to sense this and blocked my progress. I pushed ahead, forcing it to move away from the circle of light.

The other Star Crystal was only a few feet away. In a few more steps, I would be able to reach down and grab it. But the Nightshade beat me to it. It lunged for the crystal, scooped it up, and hurled it into the water.

"No!"

Sploosh! The gem hit the surface and sank. I backed up as the Nightshade picked up one large rock after another and hurled them at me. I turned to run away, dodging the flying rocks. One rock struck my knee. As I stumbled to the ground, the Star Crystal flew out of my hands and rolled across the grass.

I reached out for it, crawling. The Nightshade floated toward me. I was just inches away from the crystal when the creature's cold grip wrapped around my ankle. I kicked but the icy sensation worked its way up my leg. It had me.

Suddenly, the creature shrieked and howled. Its grip slackened and slipped off my leg. I turned to see beams of light cutting through the trees at the edge of the pond.

To my astonishment, there was Rebecca, holding a half-dozen tac lights bundled together like sticks of dynamite. I had to cover my eyes to protect them from the glare.

"The Star Crystal!" she yelled. "Turn it off, then throw it into the Nightshade and spark it up again."

"It's my only protection!"

"Do it! These batteries won't last forever."

I took a breath, grabbed the Star Crystal, muttered, "*Hap-wisk*," and threw the gem into the heart of the Nightshade.

"*Ku-fi-laz*!" I shouted.

The creature went dead still. Its form began to shudder and cracks of light appeared in its dark body. Light then began to stream out of every crack as the creature exploded into shards of shadows that flung into the air and dissolved in the daylight. Where the Nightshade once stood, Anji clutched herself in a ball, rocking back and forth.

I sprinted to my friend. "You're okay. I'm here. I'm here."

"So c-c-cold." Her teeth chattered and her skin felt like ice.

Rebecca rushed over. "She'll be okay in a few hours. We just have to keep her warm."

"You... are... working... for... Lenore." Anji pointed at Rebecca with a trembling hand.

Rebecca shook her head. "I can explain everything, but we'd better get out of here in case other Nightshades are around."

She led us through the trail and toward the mall beside the library.

"Were you following us?" I asked.

She nodded. "Someone had to keep you guys out of trouble."

"We were looking for you."

"I know. I figured that out when I saw you heading to my old foster home."

Anji asked, "Why were you following us? And why didn't you come out sooner?"

"The only way to stop Lenore Frobisher is to take away the spell page she stole. And to do that, I have to find out where she's hiding."

"So, we were bait?" I was not impressed.

"I thought I could follow the Nightshades when they reported back to her. I didn't think they would try to swallow you into the netherworld. I couldn't let that happen. Not after what you did for me."

"Oh. Well, thanks, I guess."

"We should keep moving." She glanced over her shoulder. We continued in silence until we reached a beat-up grey car in the parking lot. She opened the door, turned off the lights, and tossed her bundle of tac lights in the passenger seat. She motioned us to climb into the back seat.

Anji glanced at me. "Can we trust her?"

"I saved your life. What do you think?" Rebecca retorted.

I nodded. "Get in."

7: A New Ally

We climbed into the car while Rebecca slipped behind the steering wheel. She started the car, which took several tries before the ignition caught. Then she peeled out of the parking lot and headed onto the main road.

"Where are we going?" I asked.

Rebecca glanced back. "I want to put some distance between us and that Nightshade in case Lenore comes looking."

"How do you know so much about the Nightshades?"

"The vault contains many books and I had a lot of time on my hands. Mr. Grimoire kept asking me to charge the Star Crystals, but I never knew why. I was curious about why these gems were locked up in the vault. So I started digging into some of the old books and I learned their true purpose."

I cocked my head to the side. "And? What is that?"

"The Star Crystals aren't shields. They're meant to be used as grenades against the Nightshades.

That's why they're small enough to fit in your hand. So you can throw them."

I let out a low whistle. "I guess Mr. Grimoire doesn't know everything."

Rebecca grinned. "He likes to think he does."

She weaved in and out of traffic. I gripped my seatbelt. My stomach threatened to spew up the sushi I ate the night before.

"What about those mega-flashlights? Can they destroy Nightshades too?"

"Tac lights. They're the stuff the cops and emergency responders use. They are powerful. Put enough of these things together and you can at least hold off the monsters for a bit. But not forever."

Anji was still shivering beside me. I wrapped an arm around her and pulled her close to let my body heat warm her ice-cold skin. About fifteen minutes later, Rebecca pulled into a gas station. She filled up with gas then drove the car around to the car wash attached to the building. A couple of cars were ahead of us.

She turned off the engine and spun around. "I'm sure you're curious about what's going on."

"That's an understatement," I said.

"Lenore wants to get into the vault. I doubt Mr. Grimoire is going to step out anytime soon, so you're the next best thing. As his apprentices, you would know how to get into the vault."

"Not anymore," I said. "He changed the passwords and entrances. And Lenore might have already made her next move: Dylan's gone."

"What do you mean, *gone*? What happened to him?"

"He didn't show up to meet us this morning. I think her Nightshades must have nabbed him."

She nodded slowly. "I was watching to make sure you got home safe, Kristina. Looks as if I should have been watching Dylan."

"How can we get him back?"

"I'll have to work on a plan, but I'm afraid it might involve giving Lenore what she wants."

"What does she want?"

Rebecca looked around the parking lot as she placed her hand on the bundle of tac lights beside her. "Aleister Crowley's *Book of Spells*. The whole thing."

She looked down at her shoes.

"Of all the artefacts I told her about or showed her, this was the one that seemed to interest her the most. So many spells, so much potential for power. I showed her the book when I was trying to raise money to help my grandmother. I wanted to tease Lenore with what I had, but I didn't want her to get the book until she paid."

"Then how did she get her hands on the Nightshade spell?" Anji asked. "How can we trust you're telling the truth?"

"I owe you guys for getting the Golden Fleece for me—for my grandmother. And now that she's better, I don't need the money. And I certainly don't want to deal with Lenore anymore. I just wanted to return the favour to you and make things right. I never meant for things to get so far out of hand."

"So how did Lenore get the spell page?"

Rebecca fixed Anji with a steady gaze: "I don't know. I wish I could say I had my eye on her the whole time she was examining the book, but I must have looked away at some point, and she tore out the page."

"How did you know she had the spell?" I asked.

"After our run-in, I headed back to my hideout. I was thinking about packing up my things, grabbing my grandmother, and getting us both out of Edmonton. But I decided to lay low for a few days to let things cool off."

I narrowed my gaze at her. "You could have just left."

"Not until I paid you back. A day later, Lenore showed up. She told me she had the page and she wanted the rest of the book. She offered a huge sum for it, but I turned her down. I only took the artefacts to help my grandmother. I wasn't going to let Lenore get her hands on the book."

"So you turned her away?"

"Yes. But Lenore Frobisher doesn't take no for an answer. She wanted to know the way into the vault. I told her Mr. Grimoire would have changed the codes. She didn't believe me and tried to nab me. I escaped and I've been hiding out ever since. She must have pieced together that you guys were the new apprentices."

"What's so important about the book?" I asked. "She has the Nightshades and they seem pretty powerful. And she already seems to have all the money she needs."

Rebecca cocked her head to one side. "Money isn't everything. Lenore is all alone in the world. I remember she talked about her twin sister dying in a car accident along with their parents. She boasted about being her own boss, being independent, but I could tell she was sad and lonely."

"Was there anything in the *Book of Spells* that might help her?"

She chewed her bottom lip, then her eyes widened. "Yes. A resurrection spell. It was the one right before the summoning spell."

I clapped my hands. "Maybe she ripped out the wrong spell."

Rebecca nodded. "That would make sense. That's why she's still after the book. Maybe she wants to bring her family back to life."

"And she thinks Dylan is the key."

"Do you think he'll reveal the way into the vault?"

I shook my head. "Mr. Grimoire changed the password. Dylan has no clue."

Rebecca chewed her lip again and gazed at Anji. "Then I'm afraid he's in for a lot of pain."

I followed her gaze to my shivering friend.

"You think Lenore is going to do to him what the Nightshade tried to do to Anji?"

She nodded. "Yes, until he gives her the information she wants."

Anji sat up. "But he doesn't know anything!"

"Lenore won't know that. She'll keep sending him into the netherworld until he breaks."

"That's cruel!" Anji protested. "You don't know what it's like to be in that place. I lost myself in there. I didn't know which way was up."

"Easy." I put a hand on Anji's shoulder. "You

were only in there for a few minutes."

"It doesn't matter, Kristina. I felt like I was trapped forever."

Now it was my turn to shiver. "How long will Lenore keep it up, Rebecca? I mean, if Dylan isn't able to give her what she wants..."

She sighed. "I'm afraid she won't stop. If she's coming after you, I suspect she wants some leverage to make Dylan talk or she's going to use all of you as bait to draw Mr. Grimoire out of the vault. Either way, neither of you are safe."

"Do you know how to find her?" Anji asked. "I mean, you had to get a hold of her to let her know you had the items before. How did you communicate?"

"She gave me an unlisted number to text."

Anji nodded. "Probably a burner phone. Something that won't leave an electronic trail. We won't be able to find her with that."

I sat up. "Wait. We don't need to track her down. We just need to get in touch with her. Rebecca, can you still text Lenore a message?"

She fished her phone out of her jacket pocket. "Sure. What do you want me to text?"

"Tell her that it's from me. I want Dylan back and I'm willing to trade for him. Tell her I can get her the *Book of Spells*."

Rebecca paused. "You know what you're in for, don't you?"

"I have to save my friend."

She nodded and began to type on her phone. "Okay. Sent."

"How long does it usually take for her to reply?"

"I can't say for sure. All we can do is wait."

Rebecca dropped Anji at home so she could recover, then she drove me to my dad's place. Outside the apartment, she gave me her phone and charger.

"Why are you giving me this?"

"If Lenore is going to contact you about Dylan, I want you to be able to respond right away."

"Where are you going to be?"

She patted her bundle of flashlights. "Outside, in case she skips the phone entirely and decides to contact you another way."

I nodded. "Thanks, Rebecca."

She smiled. "You saved my grandmother. This is the least I can do."

I waved at her as I entered the apartment building and headed upstairs. Things were looking up.

8: THE DEAL

I stared at Rebecca's phone as it charged in the living room. I didn't want to miss Lenore's message. Dad was still out, and I started to wonder if he was avoiding me as well as Mom now. My stomach growled and for a couple of seconds, I eyed the hundred dollars Dad had left me, but that was it.

Instead, I checked the kitchen for something to eat. The fridge had more beer than vegetables and fruit while the cupboards were nearly bare. The only food I could find was a sleeve of saltine crackers and the dregs of peanut butter in a plastic jar.

I made myself peanut butter sandwiches with the crackers, being sure to leave the empty jar by the cash on the table so Dad knew what I had eaten. It was a petty gesture, but I hoped guilt might sway him into doing the right thing.

Still no message from Lenore. I turned my attention to going through Dad's belongings to see what else he had been spending his money on. In his bedroom, I spotted papers on the nightstand. On closer inspection, they turned out to be brochures for a resort in Mexico.

I took a closer look at the price range for the resort packages and noted that they were all over two thousand dollars. Fuming, I scanned the marks he had made on the various brochures. He had written in dates that he might be able to go and jotted notes about zip-lines and parasailing.

The jangle of keys caught my attention. I grabbed the travel brochures and stepped out of his bedroom as Dad entered. His work clothes were grimy and he dropped his box of tools on the floor beside the door. He kicked off his work boots and grinned at me. His smile dropped when he saw me holding up the travel brochures.

"I thought you said you didn't have enough money to pay Mom what you owe us. I guess you're spending it on this trip to Mexico."

"Kristina, my bedroom is off limits."

"Next time, keep the door closed. Are you really going to Mexico? Don't try to tell me *that's* for business."

He grunted before heading to the fridge. He grabbed a bottle of beer and cracked it open.

"Dad, you know how bad things are for us, don't you?"

"Kristina, I've had a long day, and I don't want to get into anything right now. Okay?"

I wasn't about to let it drop. "No, but you're happy to throw me a hundred dollars to keep quiet."

"That's for you, Kristina. Whatever you *need*, I'm always going to give it to you."

"I need you to help Mom and me out."

He picked up the cash. "I *am* helping you out."

I shook my head. "This is a handout."

"I want to make sure you get the money. I don't know if your mom is just going to blow it on her night classes or whatever else she decides to blow it on."

"She's not taking the course for fun, Dad. She's trying to get a better job so we don't have to live on top of each other in that apartment."

"Then she should learn how to budget her money better."

I couldn't believe Dad could be this cold. "Don't you care about us?"

He sat at the table and sipped the bottle. "Look, I care about you. Your mom and me... Well, we have our problems. They don't involve you."

"How can they not affect me? I'm the one sleeping on a sofa bed eating peanut butter and crackers for dinner!"

He pushed the money across the table toward me. "You don't have to."

I crossed my arms over my chest and glared.

"What else do you want me to do, Kristina?"

"Do the right thing. Be my dad and help us out. Pay your fair share!"

"I don't need a lecture from you. I had enough of that from your mom. That's why I left her in the first place."

"I thought it was because of the woman you were seeing behind her back."

Dad headed to the bedroom with his beer without another word.

I wanted to keep going, but Rebecca's phone buzzed. Lenore had responded. I checked the message.

"*Want your friend back? Bring me the book. When you have it, text me. I will send location. No tricks.*"

I replied: "*Is Dylan okay?*"

I waited a few minutes. Finally, the screen lit up with her answer.

"*Not for long. Hurry if you want to see your friends.*"

Friends? Was this a typo? My fingers trembled as I typed. "*What do you mean 'friends.'*"

I waited several minutes before the phone dinged. Instead of a message, I saw a photo of Dylan and Anji, wide-eyed and panicked.

Nightshades were wrapped around their bodies so only their shoulders and heads were visible.

My fight with Dad would have to wait. I grabbed my jacket and headed out of the apartment.

Rebecca's car was parked across the street. She slouched in the driver's seat watching me approach. She sat up as I waved the phone at her.

"I made contact. But she has Anji as well now."

Her smile faded. "I should have kept you two together."

"Lenore wants the book in exchange for my friends."

"Okay, but we can't just go to the library and find a fake one. It has to be Aleister Crowley's book and that's in the vault with Mr. Grimoire."

"If she can do this much damage with one spell, imagine what she could do with the entire book!"

"There's something that might help us," Rebecca said. "Blackwell's Phantasm Ball—the artefact that can transform into whatever you want it to be. Mr. Grimoire used it to trick me into thinking it was the Golden Fleece, remember? We can do the same to Lenore."

"But it's in the vault with Mr. Grimoire and we're out here. Do you know any other way in? We have to get him to help us."

"How do you even know he'll help you, Kristina? He's more worried about his vault than the people who work for him."

"You don't know that."

"He could have helped my grandmother with the Golden Fleece, but instead he hid it on me when I needed it."

"He's our only shot. So unless you know how to break into the vault, we're stuck with trying to convince Mr. Grimoire to play nice with us."

"Tell me what he was doing to the access points."

"Dylan was the one who helped him. He set up eyeballs as security cameras."

"Ah, the eyes in the sky. Where?"

"The fourth floor at school and an abandoned grocery store down the street."

"Okay, we'll eliminate those points. How did you get in the last time?"

"The store. But it didn't work. He locked us out."

She raised a hand. "Hold on, hold on. Let me think. The obvious access points are the stairwells. If he's moved on to the storefront, it means he's going for the access points around the school first. We might have a chance. Come with me."

I jumped into the car.

"What are you doing?"

"We're going to the farthest access point in the city."

"Where's that?"

"The Muttart Conservatory."

9: Return to the Vault

I stared through the front windshield of Rebecca's car, hoping she knew what she was doing.

"Are you sure about this entrance?" I asked. "What makes you think Mr. Grimoire hasn't locked that entry point off too?"

"It's one that he rarely remembers," she answered. "He's allergic to pollen so he doesn't think of it as a usable portal."

We arrived at the Muttart. The four tall glass pyramids in the middle of the river valley look out of place, as if a modern-day pharaoh had taken over Edmonton and set up his tombs in the middle of the city. The clouds in the sky reflected off the shiny glass.

We walked through a well-manicured garden toward a smaller fifth pyramid—the lobby. The giant sliding gate across the entrance always reminds me of the gate from an old *Jurassic Park* movie. Man, the people at the Muttart really want to protect their flowers.

We headed inside. The clerk at the desk smiled at us. "I'm sorry, but we'll be closing in half an hour."

"We only need a few minutes. My friend is working on a school project."

The clerk smiled. "Let me guess. It's due tomorrow and she only started it today."

I played the part and stared down at my shoes. "How did you know?" I muttered.

She laughed. "I have a son about your age. Go on. I won't charge, but be fast."

"Thanks," Rebecca said. She grabbed my hand and led me along the smooth, tiled path toward the hairpin hallway that led into the tropical pyramid. As soon as the automatic doors opened, a wave of humidity wrapped around me and nearly took my breath away. The temperature jumped at least fifteen degrees as we entered the jungle.

Up the incline path, a few tropical trees rose high into the air. The trail forked into two different paths. Rebecca jogged to the right, taking us past a wall of ivy wrapping around a wooden trellis.

Ahead, a tree spread its canopy over the path. Christmas lights adorned the branches. Rebecca stopped in front of the tree's plaque, which identified it as a satinwood. She glanced around the path. No one else was in the pyramid except us. She tapped the middle of the trunk six times then slid her hands down either side of the trunk to a knot near the base.

"Is this the portal?" I asked, glancing over my shoulder for any sign of security or staff. We were in the clear for now.

She twisted something at the base of the tree. The canopy, which was directly over me, closed in like an umbrella, sweeping me toward Rebecca, who stood up and pressed herself against the trunk.

For a second I thought I was going to be crushed. Suddenly, I felt weightless. I waved my arms wildly to regain my balance but I had no idea which way was up. Then I found myself on solid ground.

Beside me, Rebecca stooped behind a golden sarcophagus. Around us, other display cases showed off ancient artefacts. A few hundred feet away, stairwells rose up to nothing in mid-air. We were back in the vault!

The portal closed behind me, revealing a painting of an ancient man hanging on the wall. The nameplate read: "Dorian Gray."

Rebecca grabbed my arm and pulled me behind the giant golden sarcophagus, which was basically a coffin for mummies. She pointed to the far end of the vault where Mr. Grimoire was attaching crystals to a pole on the landing of one of the stairwells that led to nowhere.

She whispered, "He's still securing the portals. Where is Blackwell's Phantasm Ball?"

"I think it was in its display case over there. Next to Aleister Crowley's book." I pointed to the middle of the vault about a hundred feet away from Mr. Grimoire's position. There was no way we'd be able to get the ball without him noticing.

"Then we wait until he gets more supplies or he goes to sleep," she said.

I shook my head. "We don't have the time to waste."

"You want to knock him out? I don't think he'll like that."

I stared across the vault at the displays. "Wait. I have an idea. Get as close as you can to the ball and be ready."

"What are you going to do?"

"I'm going to create a distraction."

I crawled along the floor, angling away from the phantasm ball. I squeezed past a giant urn, a display case with a djinn's lamp, and a pedestal with the covered head of Medusa.

I slowed when I neared the artefact that I needed: Dr. Von Himmel's Music Box. Once I played the box's tune, I would have Mr. Grimoire under my control. I could make him forget we were ever here and then get away with the Phantasm Ball.

Only a few more feet to go and I'd have the music box. I could see the top of the box. All I had to do was stand and grab it. I started to get up but stopped when I noticed a shadow forming in front of me. I froze. Was it a Nightshade?

"Kristina?" Mr. Grimoire asked.

I rolled over in the shadow of the keeper of the vault. He held a Star Crystal in one hand and a trident in the other.

"Uh... hello, sir."

"How did you get in?"

"No time to explain, Mr. Grimoire. Dylan and Anji have been captured. We have to save them." I stood up, angling myself so that Mr. Grimoire was facing away from the Phantasm Ball.

"What do you mean? Who took them?"

"Lenore Frobisher. I need your help to free them."

"Slow down, Kristina. Tell me what happened."

"You might want to sit for this, sir." I made my way toward a stairwell, luring Mr. Grimoire farther away from Rebecca.

The old man followed. "How did you get in here?"

I lied. "Dylan showed me the portal code before he was captured."

"Which portal? I changed the codes after the

eye in the sky showed me the Nightshades lurking around the store and the stairs."

"Sir, we have to focus. Lenore is holding Anji and Dylan hostage. We have to rescue them."

"Do you know where they are being held, Kristina?"

"Lenore has a hideout in the city. We have to storm the place."

Mr. Grimoire stroked his chin, thinking. "It might be a trap."

"Mr. Grimoire, I know where she's keeping them. If we go now, we'll have the element of surprise. If we wait for her to make a move, who knows what might happen to the others?"

"That's a risk we're going to have to take."

Out of the corner of my eye, I spotted movement behind Mr. Grimoire. Rebecca was sneaking to the Phantasm Ball. I needed to keep Mr. Grimoire's focus on me for a few minutes longer.

"Sir, I'm not going to risk my friends' lives while you wait. We have to go now. We have to arm ourselves against the Nightshades."

"I need to use all the Star Crystals to secure the portals."

I shook my head. "The Star Crystals don't work that way. You have to launch them like grenades at the Nightshades."

"What? Where would you get such an idea?"

"I—I threw a crystal at one of them and it exploded. The Nightshade disappeared." He didn't need to know where I got the idea from. Not yet.

"I don't know if I have enough crystals to take down the Nightshades," he said faintly, patting his pockets as if he might find more crystals there. Clearly my news had startled him. "Who knows how many more creatures Lenore has created by now. No, the safest place is in the vault. If Lenore tries to get in, we'll be better able to defend the place."

"Anji and Dylan are out there! They risked their lives for the vault—we have to go get them!"

"I believe remaining inside is our best path."

"Don't be such a chicken!"

"Kristina!" he barked. "You may not agree with my methods, but this vault is my responsibility, and everything I do must be in service of its protection. I'm sorry about your friends, but this is what we must do."

Rebecca reached the display case and started to lift the glass off. Mr. Grimoire noticed the shift in my gaze and began to turn. I grabbed him by the arm and pulled him back toward me.

"Sir, if you don't want to leave the vault, at least give me something I can use against the Nightshades."

"I need all the Star Crystals here."

"I have to save my friends."

"No, and you're not going anywhere. This is the safest place for you as well."

Behind Mr. Grimoire, I saw Rebecca with the ball finally within her grasp, but a dark shape was rising from the floor behind her.

A Nightshade.

10: Baiting the Trap

"Look out!" I shouted.

Rebecca spun around and gasped. She backed away from the Nightshade that must have sneaked into the vault with us.

Mr. Grimoire stood frozen in horror. "They've broken in."

"Rebecca! Run!"

My partner retreated away from the Nightshade, but it wasn't interested in her. She had inadvertently led the creature to its prize: Aleister Crowley's book. It picked up the book in its skinny black hands. I started after the Nightshade, but Mr. Grimoire grabbed my arm.

"Kristina!" he hissed and pointed behind me.

Another two Nightshades rose from the floor and blocked us. I pushed Mr. Grimoire up the marble steps. The creature with the book hissed and clicked at his companions. They began to circle around the stairwell like sharks about to attack. They swung to either side of the stairwell and slithered toward us. We ran to the landing.

"You betrayed me!" he said accusingly.

"Are you nuts? I had no idea they were following us."

Mr. Grimoire reached for the crystals mounted on the railing, but the Nightshades were quicker, batting them to the floor below. We were trapped. The Nightshade with the book joined its allies as they closed in on us. I stood in front of my mentor, shielding him from the cold void that was about to wrap around us.

"*Ku-fi-laz!*"

The Nightshade nearest to us stiffened.

Cracks of light appeared in its chest as it began to shudder. Then it burst into a thousand dark shards. The other creatures whirled around. At the bottom of the stairwell, Rebecca held her bundle of tac lights.

"Cover your eyes!"

I shielded my eyes from the high-intensity light that burst from the tac lights. The Nightshades screeched, their hideous wails sounding like fingernails scraping across an old blackboard.

One creature leapt off the stairwell, howling as it crashed on top of Rebecca, knocking her down. The bundle of tac lights skidded across the floor. I had to help her before the creature swallowed her into the void. The Nightshade with the book advanced on us.

"Mr. Grimoire, stay here."

I hopped on the banister and slid down, zipping past the outstretched black arm of the Nightshade. I landed on the marble floor a few feet away from the Nightshade now covering most of Rebecca's body. Only her face was visible and her eyes bulged in pain. I scanned the floor and spotted what I needed: two Star Crystals.

I lunged for them both and hurled one into the Nightshade on top of Rebecca, then clutched the other one to my chest as the third creature wrapped itself around me. The cold bit into my bones as it enveloped my body.

"*Ku-fi-laz*!" I gasped.

The Nightshade on top of me screeched as its body splintered into a thousand dark shards, then it was gone. The book flopped on the floor, released from the creature's grip. Beside me, Rebecca dusted herself off, no longer a captive of the other Nightshade that had exploded at the same time.

"I think it's safe now," I said.

I held my hand out to Rebecca to pull her off the floor. Her hand was ice cold.

"What did you do?" Mr. Grimoire asked in amazement, coming down the steps and scooping up the book.

"I tried to tell you, sir. The crystals are grenades."

"Well, I see that now." Mr. Grimoire cocked his head and glared at Rebecca. "How on earth did you get in here?"

"I was an attentive apprentice, sir. We came in through the Muttart."

He growled. "I knew I'd forgotten one entrance."

"Sorry, sir, but we needed to get into the vault, and you weren't letting us in," I explained.

"Because I didn't want you to bring those *things* in. They almost got away with the *Book of Spells*. And I certainly didn't want *her* in the vault."

"Sir, Rebecca is our best shot against the Nightshades. She's the one who told me how to defeat them," I said. "We need her help to get Dylan and Anji back."

"You can't trust that girl," he said, still staring coldly at Rebecca.

She returned his glare. "You care more about the things in this place than the people in your life."

"The artefacts are not meant for your whims."

"That's why you're alone, and that's why you've never been able to keep an apprentice."

"You betrayed me."

"I was trying to save my grandmother, and you had the means to do it. Why wouldn't you let me help her?"

"The world isn't ready to see what I have collected."

"Mr. Grimoire, isn't this why the vault was created in the first place? It's not a locked box. It's an archive for people to view and study."

"I'll decide what the vault is for. Not you."

"And you'd rather horde all of this to yourself. Selfish old man."

I stepped in between the two of them. "Listen to me. Enough."

They stepped back from each other.

"He's a stubborn fool."

"Both of you are thick-headed. Mr. Grimoire, I know what Rebecca did was wrong, but she was trying to help her grandmother. She was protecting what was most important to her, just as you were protecting what was most important to you."

"His artefacts," Rebecca said.

I shook my head. "He was trying to protect you. He didn't want to risk losing you, but he's been the keeper of the vault so long, the only way he knew how to protect you was to keep you inside here."

She stared at her mentor. "Is Kristina right?"

He returned her gaze. "She barely knows us."

"The truth, sir. Tell Rebecca. I can see it in your eyes. You care for her."

He walked away from her. "I don't know what she's talking about. I needed an apprentice. That's all. Now I have you, Kristina. What do I need her for?"

"Do you really believe that, sir?"

He kept his back to us and said nothing.

"Sir?"

Finally, he spoke. "My apprentices were always curious and greedy. They wanted these treasures for themselves. You never did, or at least I thought you never did. Then you stole from me the very things you swore to protect."

"I'm sorry for that. I was desperate."

"I thought you were different, but you're like all the others. Leaving me alone."

"You're not alone now, Mr. Grimoire," I said. "She came back for you."

"To steal more."

Rebecca shook her head. "No, to get back what should have never left the vault. The page from Aleister Crowley's book. I never should have shown Lenore the spells. Give me the chance to make things right."

"I trusted you once. Never again."

I piped up. "I trust Rebecca, sir. She saved my life twice. She didn't have to help me get back to the vault. She could have run off to join her grandmother, but she stayed."

"Why?" he asked.

"Ever since my parents died and I ran away from my grandmother, I've bounced from foster family to foster family," Rebecca said. "The people who looked after me were nice, but I never felt like I belonged there. This vault is where I feel like I'm home, sir. And it's because of you. I didn't want to disappoint you again."

Mr. Grimoire's expression did not change. "I wish I could believe you."

"I'm sorry, sir. I truly am. I didn't mean to cause all of this."

"Mr. Grimoire," I interrupted. "We can sort this out later, but right now we have two other apprentices we have to save. They risked their lives for your collection. Are you going to help me get Anji and Dylan back?"

He paused for a moment and then sighed. "We'll need more crystals—and you will do as I tell you. Understood?"

We nodded and then got to work.

We spent the next hour gathering the Star Crystals from the stairwells and placing them in a sack. No matter how many of the gems we stuffed inside, the bottomless bag never seemed to fill up.

Rebecca grinned. "We call it Benton's Bag. I say it's a girl's best friend—a bag that holds everything."

"Not much in the fashion department," I said.

"But it's practical," she said.

"How does it work?"

Mr. Grimoire explained, "Legend has it that Benton was a wizard around the time before Robin Hood. He would steal from the rich farmers. He disguised himself as a merchant, and he claimed he had all manner of wares within his sack. In truth, he filled it with food that he could give to the poor. No one suspected him because no one ever thought the sack could hold that much. Benton pushed the few people who dared to check its contents right into the bag, and they were never seen or heard from again."

"What if we used Dr. Von Himmel's Music Box?" I suggested. "Turn the crank, let the music play, and Lenore will be under our control."

"Not a good idea," Rebecca said. "When I

took the artefacts, I told Lenore what they could do. She'd be ready for the music box."

"Then how do we capture her?"

Mr. Grimoire picked up a golden pin from a display case. It looked like a sideways number eight—the symbol for infinity. "The Mobius Strip might come in handy for this situation."

I jumped in. "You mean that thing that loops around itself forever?"

He nodded, "Whoever is on the receiving end of the Mobius Strip will be trapped. The strip loops around to the beginning no matter which direction you move. It's an eternal prison."

"Perfect," Rebecca said.

Mr. Grimoire pinned the golden infinity symbol to his lapel.

"What's the plan, sir?" I asked.

"You two had a good idea with the Phantasm Ball. We'll make Lenore think you have the book. What she won't know is that you'll also have Rebecca and me lurking in the wings ready to rescue Anji and Dylan."

"But what about the Nightshades? She might have an army of them by now. I don't think we have enough Star Crystals."

"I have a workaround solution. Kristina, can you put the rest of the crystals in the bag?"

"I can do it," Rebecca offered.

"I asked my apprentice." He glared at her.

"No problem, sir," I said as I scooped the gems into the sack.

Mr. Grimoire set the sack in the middle of the floor and pulled me back. "Look away from the sack. This is going to get very bright," he warned us. "*Ku-fi-laz.*"

From the corner of my eye, I saw a brilliant flash of light erupting from the middle of the bag and shooting straight up. Mr. Grimoire reached into his pocket and pulled out a prism about the size of a harmonica. He shoved the prism into the middle of the light. Multiple beams of light cascaded around the vault, filling every nook and cranny. I shielded my eyes as the light bathed me in its hot glow. I felt like I was at the beach getting a blistering sunburn.

"*Hap-wisk.*"

Cool air returned. The vault seemed so much dimmer now.

Mr. Grimoire pocketed the prism. "That was the Prism of Persia, a trinket I picked up many years ago. I never had thought to use it in this way. Originally, it was a means to make the most of a little light. I had never thought to amplify it like this until now."

Rebecca nodded. "That's a thousand times more intense than the crystals. It should banish the Nightshades."

"That is my hope. Kristina, what arrangements have you made with Lenore for contacting her?"

I pulled the phone out of my pocket. "I'm supposed to let her know when I have the book and she'll give me the meeting location."

"Are you ready?" he asked.

Rebecca and I nodded. I typed a message and pressed send.

A few minutes later, the phone pinged with a link to a map. I clicked on the link. On the screen, a map brought up Fort Edmonton, the historical site in the river valley.

"Okay," I said. "Now or never."

11: LIGHTS OUT

We had an hour to get to Fort Edmonton, but at the rate Mr. Grimoire was driving we'd be lucky if we showed up by the end of the week.

Rebecca sat in the passenger seat, nervously rubbing the shoulder strap of her seatbelt.

"I could drive, Mr. Grimoire."

"No. I'm fine."

"We'd get there faster."

"Let Lenore wait. I want to get there in one piece."

"I'd like to get there while I'm still young."

As Mr. Grimoire and Rebecca bickered, I stared out the window, trying to figure out how to rescue our friends. If they were inside a building, we might have a chance of scrubbing out the Nightshades, but if they were outside, the Nightshades could hide among the buildings. Plus, we had to worry about the tourists in the park. So many things could go wrong.

Mr. Grimoire parked a few hundred feet away from the tollbooth that marked the entrance to the Fort. He let us out so we could head to the front entrance while he drove to the service road that led to the back of the Fort. He was our backup, and we had to give him enough time to find us.

Shadows surrounded us. I kept peeking behind me, half-expecting an ambush.

Rebecca patted my arm and joked, "I bet we'll still get into the Fort faster than him."

I nodded but said nothing.

"And we'd have time for tea."

I forced a smile. "Yes."

"Your friends will be okay, Kristina."

When we approached the gate, I was surprised to see no one manning the booths. The staff was gone, even though the sign showed that the Fort was still open.

"I think Lenore's beaten us here," I said.

Rebecca reached into her pack to pull out her bundle of tac lights. "Go. I don't want Lenore to see me. Let her think you're alone."

"Stay close."

"I will. Keep your eyes open. If she's outside, try to move the meeting inside a building."

I nodded as I pulled the Phantasm Ball out of my backpack and whispered, "Aleister Crowley's *Book of Spells*." The artefact transformed into the heavy, old book.

Rebecca nodded at the illusion. "Not bad. I'd fall for it."

"Let's hope Lenore does as well."

I strolled into the main area of the Fort, slipping back into history. The City of Edmonton had relocated several older buildings to the fort area to mark off the city's evolution through the eras. One street was filled with buildings from the time when Edmonton had been a trading fort. Another street showed buildings from the early 1900s.

I felt as if eyes were watching me from every structure as I surveyed either side of the street. But there was no sign of life anywhere.

I had to buy Mr. Grimoire enough time to get to the back of the Fort. I tried not to look back for Rebecca. It had to appear as if I were facing Lenore alone.

At the end of a street, a two-storey white storefront waited for me. A light was on in one of the main floor windows. The sign over the door read: "Kelly's Saloon." I stopped about thirty paces away from the building and scanned the area for Nightshades. Plenty of shadows, but I couldn't tell if they were the creatures or not.

The saloon door opened and Lenore stepped out. "You took your sweet time."

"Where are my friends?" I asked.

"Do you have what I wanted?"

I held up the fake book.

She smiled. "Give me the book."

"No way. Not until I see my friends."

"You don't trust me?"

"That tends to happen when you kidnap people."

Lenore shrugged. "Fine, fine. Have it our way." She snapped her fingers.

The Nightshades slithered from a dark corner, carrying with them the figures of Anji and Dylan. They gasped for air as they were pinned against the monsters like butterflies mounted on a board. The creatures surrounded me. There had to be at least twenty of them.

"Satisfied?" Lenore asked.

"Now let them go. I brought what you wanted."

She crossed her arms. "Or else what, dear?"

"Or else you don't get the book."

She laughed. "You're in no position to utter threats, dear. Not when I can do this." She snapped her fingers.

Dylan howled in pain as the Nightshade that was holding him began to split apart, pulling at my friend's limbs as if he were on a torture rack.

"Okay, okay. You win," I shouted. "Let's go inside. I'll give you what you want."

She snapped her fingers, and the Nightshade merged back around Dylan and carried him into the saloon. The other creatures followed suit. I waited, trying to scan the area for Rebecca and Mr. Grimoire.

Lenore cocked her head to one side. "If you're thinking of making a run for it, don't. It won't end well if you do."

I shuffled to the doorway. The Nightshades closed in around me, herding me inside with Lenore and my friends.

Wooden tables and chairs filled the middle of the room and a bar counter stood at the back. Lenore leaned against the counter while her monsters set the captives at a round table near one of the windows.

I glanced back at the Nightshades crowded in the doorway and drew them in, stepping into the middle of the saloon. The trap was set. The rest was up to Mr. Grimoire and Rebecca.

"Now give me the book," Lenore said.

"Let my friends go first and you can have it."

"Do you take me for a fool? I want to examine the merchandise first."

I gaped at the Nightshades surrounding me.

103

I had to stall a little longer.

"Let Anji go as a sign of good faith."

Lenore smiled. "That's not the way it works, dear. I get the book first, then you get your friends."

She motioned to the Nightshades. They began to crowd around me. I reached into my pocket and pulled out a Star Crystal.

"Stay back!" I ordered.

The creatures hesitated. I waved the crystal, warding off the enemies closing the circle around me.

"You're delaying the inevitable, dear. I have what I want, and there is nothing you can do about it."

Through the window, I caught a glimpse of movement. That had to be Mr. Grimoire and Rebecca.

I inched toward Anji and Dylan. The Nightshades closed in on me.

"Now!" I screamed, hoping to cue Rebecca and Mr. Grimoire.

They entered the saloon but not the way I had hoped. Two Nightshades held my partners in their tarry arms as they slinked into the room.

"Ah, Mr. Grimoire. Rebecca. So good to see you again. Unfortunate that it had to come to this.

I'm assuming the real book is not here and you're just carrying a decoy?"

I glared at her, refusing to give her the satisfaction of an answer.

"No matter. I have the keeper of the vault. I'm sure he'll let me in and get the book."

"Never," Mr. Grimoire growled.

"It's not worth it, Lenore," Rebecca said. "You'll never get Lana back!"

Her eyes widened with surprise. "What? How did you..."

"So I was right. You want your sister Lana back among the living."

"She's my twin. I'd do anything for her."

"What price are you willing to pay?" I asked.

"Whatever it takes."

Mr. Grimoire pleaded. "The spell comes with serious consequences, Lenore. You can't do this."

She took a breath, regaining a mask of calm. "I will do as I please."

"I'm not giving up the vault to you." Mr. Grimoire struggled helplessly.

"You will, my friend, you will."

"Let him go," I ordered. "Or else everything you want will go up in a puff of smoke."

Lenore hesitated.

I pressed my luck as a new plan began to take

shape in my mind. "We prepared for this scenario. Mr. Grimoire rigged the vault to explode all the portals if he was captured. If he doesn't return in three hours, the collection will be lost forever."

She turned to Mr. Grimoire. "You'd risk losing your precious artefacts? I find that hard to believe."

Mr. Grimoire stared at me for a moment before answering. "Better than having them in your hands."

"You have no choice," Rebecca added. "We can wait you out and you'll lose."

Lenore ignored her. She strode to Mr. Grimoire. "How do you disarm the trap?"

"As Kristina said: I return to the vault."

She shook her head. "I don't believe you. If you were delayed somehow, you'd have a failsafe."

"Don't tell her!" I blurted out, shooting Mr. Grimoire a look.

He caught on and shook his head. "There is no failsafe, Lenore. Don't listen to Kristina."

Lenore advanced on me. "Where is it, Kristina?"

"I'll never tell you."

Lenore snapped her fingers at the Nightshade holding the keeper of the vault. "What did he have with him?"

The Nightshade tossed the Benton bag

across the wooden floor, along with the Mobius Strip and the Prism of Persia, which they must have found in Mr. Grimoire's pockets.

"They are nothing," Mr. Grimoire said, struggling.

She beamed. "I'm not familiar with these artefacts, but I suspect you intended to use them as weapons against me. How quaint. I'll add them to my growing collection. Now let's see what wonders you've brought me." She stooped over the sack and began to unknot the drawstring.

"There's nothing here," she said.

"That's what you think," I said, inching closer toward her and the sack.

A Nightshade stepped in front of me. I held up the "book" and whispered, "Star Crystal."

The book morphed into a crystal and I held it out in front of me. The Nightshade shrank back in fear.

Lenore pulled out a handful of Star Crystals. "What are these?"

This was my chance to act. I hurled the fake crystal at the Nightshade, forcing it to slide out of the way, clearing a path to Lenore.

I charged ahead and threw myself at Lenore, grabbing the Star Crystals in her hands. We pulled back and forth for a moment, like a tug-of-war, but I had my hands on them.

"*Ku-fi-laz*!" I screamed as I shut my eyes.

The room exploded with heat. Lenore's screams filled the air and she let go.

I opened my eyes, squinting. Lenore was covering her face. The other Nightshades had retreated to the corners and released Anji and Dylan. They dropped to their knees gasping for air. Mr. Grimoire climbed to his feet and staggered toward the sack.

Lenore clutched her head, still reeling from the blinding flash. I tried to grab the Prism of Persia, but a Nightshade grabbed my legs. Icy pain shot up and down my calves.

"The Prism!" Mr. Grimoire shouted.

"Send Grimoire to the netherworld!" Lenore shrieked.

A cluster of Nightshades charged at him, but Rebecca threw herself in front of their path.

"Get the Prism!" she yelled as the creatures swallowed her body. Her shrieks filled the air as they coiled around her.

Mr. Grimoire stepped back, stunned by Rebecca's action. Two more Nightshades advanced on him from either side.

Dylan staggered forward and scooped up the Prism while Anji grabbed the Mobius Strip.

"Anji!" Mr. Grimoire yelled. "Throw that at Lenore."

She rifled the pin at Lenore and Mr. Grimoire commanded, "*Vistressia!*" as the pin flew across the room.

Lenore looked up in time to see the glowing infinity symbol. She raised her arms defensively— then she just winked out of existence. The Mobius Strip floated in the air where she once stood.

Still, the Nightshades tore at Mr. Grimoire and me.

"What do I do with this thing?" Dylan asked, waving the Prism over his head.

"Shove it into the light beams!" I shouted, grimacing from the cold creeping up my body.

Dylan dodged a Nightshade and thrust the Prism into one of the beams of light shooting out of the crystals in my outstretched hands. Like a disco ball catching a spotlight, the beam exploded and shot around the room.

The Nightshades wailed in pain as the light struck them. Their forms exploded into shards of darkness. The creatures' eerie shrieks filled the room like a thousand banshees screaming at once.

Then everything went silent.

I stared around the room. There was no sign of the enemy—only the keeper of the vault and his apprentices, including Rebecca, gasping for air on the floor.

"*Hap-wisk*," I ordered.

The light faded. Dylan crawled over to check on Anji. "You okay?"

She moaned, "I'm not Snow White and you're not Prince Charming. Now get your onion breath out of my face."

I laughed and clapped Dylan on the back. "You came in useful for a change."

He beamed.

Mr. Grimoire helped Rebecca to her feet. "Are you all right?"

She nodded. "Did it work?"

He placed his hand on her shoulder. "Yes. Thanks to you."

12: Endings and Beginnings

It didn't take Mr. Grimoire long to discover where Lenore had hidden the spell page. We found her black car in the parking lot. The missing page was in a briefcase in the car's trunk.

We piled into Mr. Grimoire's car and drove back to the school. Once we were all in the vault, Mr. Grimoire placed the Mobius Strip on a table beside Dr. Von Himmel's Music Box. He picked up a jar of wax and handed it to me.

"Cover your ears," he ordered.

We obeyed and filled our ears with the sound-blocking wax.

Mr. Grimoire motioned to us to step back. We did so and watched as he picked up the music box and turned the crank. Then he put the box down and said something directed at the Mobius Strip.

The sideways eight glimmered, growing brighter until it flashed. I blinked away the spots from the flash. Lenore stood before us. She was ramrod still.

Mr. Grimoire indicated that we could clean the wax out of our ears.

"What are you going to do with her?" I asked.

"You'll see, Kristina." He turned to Lenore. "From this moment on, you'll remember nothing of the vault, the book, or any of our dealings. You will go back to your life as if you were on a long vacation."

"I will remember nothing," she said dreamily.

Dylan piped up. "And make sure she never comes back to Edmonton."

Anji shook her head. "You should have left her on the Mobius Strip after what she did to us." She shivered.

"What about Rebecca?" I said. "Are you going to wipe out her memory?"

The keeper of the vault looked at Rebecca for a long moment. "What you did back there, you did without a thought to your own safety. I owe you a debt, Rebecca."

"I would do anything for you, sir."

"That is well and good because we have much work ahead of us—my apprentice."

"What? Wait. I thought we were your new apprentices. Are you firing us?" I asked. "After what we did for you?"

He shook his head. "I'm sorry, Kristina. I'm afraid I wasn't clear. I'm not relieving you of your duties. I'm giving the three of you new tasks."

"Doing what?" asked Dylan.

"We have to find a way to introduce the artefacts to the world, slowly and carefully. You will be the ambassadors. You have to find more people like you, people who are curious about the wonders of the world, but are also responsible enough not to abuse their powers."

"You're opening the vault?" I asked incredulously.

"Not all at once. I still don't think the entire world is ready, but if the three of you are any indication, I believe there are some people who understand the responsibilities of the collection, and I need you to find them."

Dylan straightened up. "I think I know a few people who might fit the bill."

Anji cocked her head to one side. "Why the change of heart?"

Mr. Grimoire glanced at Rebecca. "If what we have in this collection can bring some good to the world, I cannot deny access to the vault. My stubbornness nearly cost me a dear friend. I won't make that mistake twice."

I took a long look at Mr. Grimoire. "You're sure you want us to do this?"

"I have faith you'll find the right people. You seem to be a good judge of character, after all."

I smiled.

"Kristina, you and your friends will always be keepers of the vault. You've proven yourselves loyal. And so has Rebecca. I need all of your talents and your help to protect the vault and to help it reach its full potential."

"Count me in."

"What Dylan said," Anji quipped.

Mr. Grimoire turned to me. "Well?"

"I wouldn't miss it for the world."

He held out his hand to shake mine, but I hugged him instead. Then my friends and I headed out of the vault.

Outside the school, we made our way to the bus stop.

Dylan joked, "School is never going to be this exciting ever again."

"I don't know. English class might be thrilling."

He groaned.

Anji quipped, "Mr. Carlton? You want to hear his tales of being a published author again? And again?"

Dylan laughed. "And again."

"I don't even know where to start or who to ask."

Anji smiled. "Trust your gut. And don't forget I've got access to the Dark Web. I can do a background check on everyone and anyone."

"Okay. I'll see you guys at school next week."

"I'm sleeping for a week. Under two blankets with heating pads," Dylan said.

"Sounds like a plan," Anji said.

We parted company and I returned to Dad's place, dreading seeing him more than my run-in with Lenore and the Nightshades.

At Dad's apartment, he was waiting for me. My suitcase was packed.

"Where were you?" he grunted.

"I needed some air."

He shook his head. "You live under my roof, you live by my rules. Curfew means something. After ten, you are to be inside. Do you understand?"

I nodded. "Why is the suitcase packed?"

"I thought you would want to go back to your mother's place."

"Decided I'm too much trouble?" I said. "Don't want to spend any more of your Mexico money looking after me?"

"What's it going to take for you to drop this?"

"Pay Mom."

"You know that money's tight for me, too, right? I'm a freelancer. Sometimes, I get work.

Sometimes, I don't. And I have to pay for my equipment and supplies."

"And your truck. And your Oilers' tickets. And your vacations."

"So what if I spend a little on myself now and then? It's not like your mom's a saint. She's blowing your money on her night classes. If she didn't take those courses, she'd be able to work more and have enough to look after herself."

"Are you kidding?" I shot back. "She's practically killing herself with work. She's taking those classes so she can make enough money to take care of me. Like you're supposed to be doing because you already can."

He said nothing. Instead, he picked up my suitcase and headed to the door.

"Where are you going with that?"

"Taking you home. Let's go."

I followed him to his new truck and climbed in. We rode in silence for the first part of the trip. I didn't know what else I could do to get Dad to own up and admit he was wrong.

He parked in front of Mom's apartment building and sat behind the steering wheel. I started to reach for the door handle.

"Wait, Kristina."

"What?"

"You know you'll always be welcome at my house, and I'll never stop being your dad."

"I know."

"But your mom and me, well, we're still trying to figure out who we are to each other."

"I get that, Dad. It's hard for her, too."

He reached into his pocket and pulled out a chequebook. "Well, this might make it a little easier." He filled out a cheque and handed it to me.

The cheque was made out to Mom and the amount was enough to cover most of our bills. I looked back at Dad.

"Really?"

He nodded. "If you're not getting what you need, you'll let me know, right?"

"Yes, Dad. I will."

I opened the truck door and stepped out. I paused. "Dad?"

"Yeah?"

"Thanks."

I headed into the apartment, wheeling my suitcase behind me. I glanced back at Dad, sitting in his new truck. He waved. I nodded and entered the building. He had his faults, but he was still my dad. I was glad he was starting to act like one.

In our apartment, Mom was slumped over her textbook at the kitchen table, sleeping. She needed her rest. I gently slipped Dad's cheque under her elbow. Then I walked over to the sofa and pulled out my bed and sheets.

So much had changed since my parents split up. A new apartment, a different school, new friends—and the biggest change of all—a strange vault with the wonders of the world.

I didn't know if I'd be ready for the changes Mr. Grimoire had in store. But then again, when Mom and Dad broke up, I didn't think I'd be ready to deal with that either. If I could cope with their divorce and life at a new school, I figured I could manage being a keeper of the vault, no matter what that role was. Either way, I couldn't wait to see what tomorrow would bring.

Also by Marty Chan:

Keepers of the Vault

Fire and Glass

Melody and Myth

Marty Chan Mysteries

Mystery of the Frozen Brains

Mystery of the Graffiti Ghoul

Mystery of the Cyber-bully

Mystery of the Mad Science Teacher

Ehrich Weisz Chronicles

Infinity Coil

Demon Gate

Marty Chan writes books for kids and plays for adults. He's best known for his **Marty Chan Mystery** series. When he's not writing, he's practising stage magic for his school presentations. For more information, please visit martychan.com.

Read an interview with Marty about the **Keepers of the Vault** series at clockwisepress.com.